D1244504

I dedicate this book to my parents, Barry and Gloria.

www.mascotbooks.com

For more information, please contact:
Mascot Books
560 Herndon Parkway #120
Herndon, VA 20170
info@mascotbooks.com

Library of Congress Control Number: 2012948553

CPSIA Code: PRT1112A
ISBN: 1620861437
ISBN-13: 9781620861431

Printed in the United States

MOM! WHAT'S THAT?

By Atlas Jordan
Illustrated by Barry Jordan Jr.

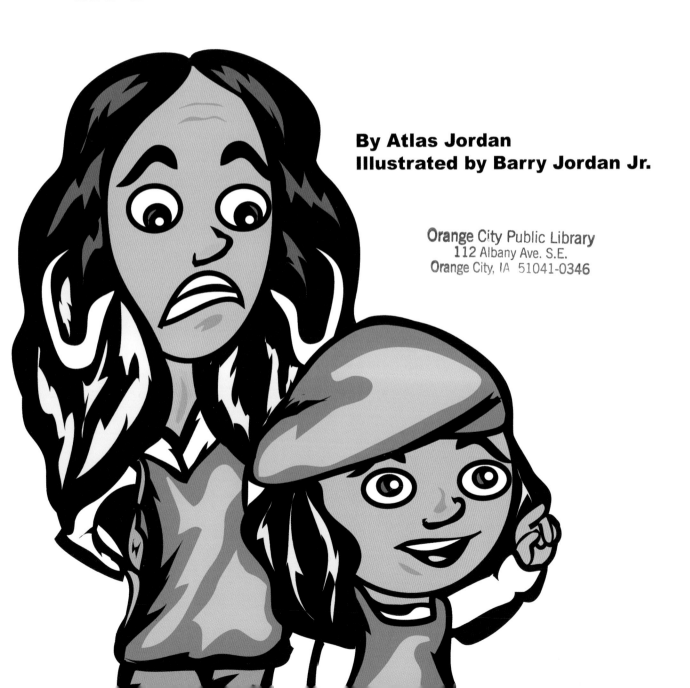

Mom and Sadie were having fun walking down the street today. Sadie became very excited when Mom thought of a "who and what" game to play.

As they approached the end of the street,

all of a sudden, Mom and Sadie paused. They

saw an animal that had whiskers and four claws.

"Sadie, what's that?" asked Mom.

"That's a cat!"

"What color is he?"

"The cat is black."

As Mom and Sadie crossed the street, they saw a creature that looked rather strange. Part of the creature was wrapped in newspaper and the rest of it looked to be plain.

Sadie became so frightened that mom

knew what she was going to say.

Mom and Sadie headed toward the park.

Some kids were standing on the mound.

As they were setting up for baseball

practice, Sadie wondered who was making

that popping sound.

"Every time he hits the ball with the beige bat, it makes loud sounds that go *smack! crack!* and *whack!*"

The noise scared off the black cat, which had been chasing the gray rat.

Mom and Sadie sat down on the bleachers.

They stayed and watched the game for awhile.

When the next batter came up to the plate

to hit, Sadie burst out with a smile.

"Sadie, who's that?"

"That's my brother Matt. It looks like he's

wearing a plastic hat."

"Mom, who's that?"

"That's our neighbor, Nat. Earlier, he had tripped over the black cat. Now he has gotten hit in the leg by Matt when he let go of the baseball bat. The coach is trying to contact his mother, Pat."

Sadie and Mom were heading home after sharing their day at the park. They were trying to reach their destination before the daylight began to turn dark.

Mom and Sadie stopped at a bakery shop.
It displayed all kinds of cookies, cakes,
and pies.

Sadie was wiggling, giggling, and doing
a happy dance. She could not believe
her eyes.

"Mom, who's that?"

"That's Mr. Fats. He is the owner of the

Pastry Rack."

Sadie asked Mom if she would buy

some doughnuts or sweet

potato jacks.

"I remember seeing the black cat who chased the gray rat. The coach's son Jack hit the ball with a beige bat. The sounds of the hit were *smack! crack!* and *whack!*

"Then, there was brother, Matt, who was wearing a plastic hat. Then, he threw the bat and hit our neighbor, Nat. The coach had to call his mother, Pat. We stopped at Mr. Fat's Pastry Rack and bought some sweet potato jacks."

Mom was very proud of Sadie.

She had learned so much today.

They went on inside their house to stay.

About the Author

Atlas Jordan grew up in Chesapeake, Virginia. As a young student, he received a Certificate of Achievement Award and a Certificate of Merit from the Virginia State Reading Association, Young Authors Program. Throughout his school years, he was on the Principal's Honor Roll and he graduated from Deep Creek High School as an honor student. He also graduated with honors from Norfolk State University in Norfolk, Virginia. There, he received his Bachelor of Arts in Psychology. In May 2012, he received his Master's Degree in Social Work from Norfolk State University.